The Joker

When Adam and Sue got back from school on Friday afternoon, Mum had some news for them, 'Our new neighbours moved in this morning,' she said. 'They seem to be very friendly.'

'Have they any children?' asked Adam.

'Yes,' replied Mum. 'I saw a little boy called Alex. I think he's about your age. I expect he'll be going to your school.'

'Can we go and say hello?' asked Sue.

'When you've had your tea,' said Mum.

1

After tea Adam and Sue went to the neighbours'
house. A boy opened the door.

'Hello,' said Sue. 'You must be Alex. I'm Sue
and this is my brother, Adam. We're your next door
neighbours.'

'Good,' said Alex. 'I hope we're going to be
friends. I don't know anybody around here.'

Alex told them he would be starting at their school on Monday. 'I suppose it will take me a while to get used to things. I liked my school in Newcastle,' he said. 'What's yours like?'

'I think you'll like it,' said Adam. 'We do. Most of the time.'

'It's Saturday tomorrow,' said Sue. 'Come to our house in the morning and we'll take you up to Uncle Brian's farm.'

When Alex arrived the next morning Adam was just
starting to wash the car. It was how he earned
his pocket money. 'I have to finish this job,'
he said. 'But Sue will be out in a minute. She'll
take you to the farm, and I'll come later.'

'That sounds like a good idea,' said Alex. 'I'll
go and put my wellies on and be back in a minute.'

'Where's Alex?' asked Sue, coming out of the house.

'Putting his wellingtons on,' said Adam. 'You take
him up to the farm. I'll come when I've finished.'

4

When Alex came back he had a big smile on his face.

'Is something funny?' asked Sue.

'Oh no,' said Alex. 'I think I'm ready to go to the farm now.'

'You can meet our cousin, Carla,' said Sue. 'She'll probably let you have a go on Zebedee. And I'm sure you'll like Max and Jet.'

'I suppose Zebedee must be a pony,' said Alex. 'But who are Max and Jet? Are they your cousins too?'

'No,' laughed Sue. 'Max and Jet are the farm dogs.'

Alex seemed to like everything on the farm. He soon
made friends with Carla, Max and Jet but he seemed
nervous of Zebedee.

'Have you never ridden a pony before?' asked Carla.

'I had a few lessons at my last school,' said Alex,
'but I wasn't very good at it. I do like horses but
they seem to know that I'm nervous of them.'

Zebedee was in a paddock at the back of a farmhouse.

'You can watch me take him over the jumps,' said Carla. 'Then you can have a ride yourself if you like.'

Sue could see that Alex was worried. 'Zebedee is very gentle,' she said. 'You'll be fine once you get used to him.'

'I'd like to have a try,' said Alex, 'but I must warn you that I'm pretty hopeless.'

Carla was a good rider. She rode Zebedee around the
paddock a few times. Then she took him over the
jumps. They were not very difficult jumps
but Alex still looked nervous. 'I hope she doesn't
expect me to do that,' he said to Sue. 'I find it
hard enough to stay on when the horse isn't moving.'

    'You don't have to do anything you don't want to,'
said Sue. 'Carla has been riding for years. She
wouldn't expect you to go over the jumps.'

Sue rode Zebedee next and then it was Alex's turn.
Carla held the pony's bridle and Sue helped Alex get
on his back. Almost at once Alex began to slip. He
held on to the pony's neck and slithered off the
other side. It was a long time before he managed
to get both his feet in the stirrups and sit upright.

'I told you I was hopeless,' he said.

'Everybody has to start somewhere,' said Carla.

Adam came into the paddock to watch. Carla tried to lead Zebedee but he only walked three paces before Alex fell off again.

'Never mind,' said Adam, 'Uncle Brian has asked us to stay for lunch. We'd better go and eat.'

Everybody enjoyed their lunch. Alex had second
helpings of everything. 'I hope you don't think I am
being greedy,' he said, 'but falling off horses
always makes me hungry.'

'You go right ahead,' laughed Uncle Brian. 'I eat
like a horse myself and I like to see others enjoying
their food. If people didn't eat their dinners,
farmers like me would be out of a job!'

'Mum suggested we go to the circus this afternoon,' said Adam. 'She's given me enough money for us all to go.'

'That's great!' said Carla. 'I love circus horses.'

'I don't know!' said Uncle Brian. 'Don't you ever think about anything but horses, Carla?'

'Of course I do,' replied Carla. 'Sometimes I think about ponies.'

'I'll have to go home first,' said Alex, 'to tell my parents where I'm going.'

When it was time to go to the circus, Adam, Sue
and Carla went to call for Alex. They were amazed
to see that he was just finishing an enormous meal.

'Alex!' gasped Sue. 'Where do you put it all?'

'Yes,' said Adam. 'You've just had a huge meal at
Uncle Brian's.'

'I've always had a good appetite,' said Alex,
with a mischievous smile, 'I can eat enough for two.'

The circus was good fun. Adam liked the clowns best. But Sue and Carla liked the horses. One of the clowns came into the centre of the ring to make an announcement.

'Ladies and Gentlemen,' he said. 'Our next act is the amazing Cossack riders. You will see stunts on horseback that you will not believe. And when the act is over I shall invite one of you to have a go. No harm will come to you. We have a special harness that makes it impossible for you to fall off.'

The Cossack riders were amazing. They galloped around the ring standing on the backs of their horses. Some of them did handstands. Some jumped from one horse to another.

'I bet I could do that,' said Alex.
Everybody laughed.

17

When the act was over the clown came back into the ring. 'Now, ladies and gentlemen,' he said. 'Is there anyone brave enough to have a go?'

'Yes,' said Alex, and he began to walk towards the ring.

'Come back!' shouted Carla. 'You can't even sit on a horse, let alone stand.'

'Don't worry,' said Adam. 'I've seen this trick before. He'll just go flying around the ring on the safety harness, and everybody will laugh at him.'

The clown helped Alex into the saddle.

'That's funny,' said Sue. 'It looks as if he knows what he's doing.'

The horse began to trot slowly around the ring. Then it began to gallop. Alex stayed in the saddle. Then he stood up on the horse's back.

'I can't believe it!' gasped Adam. 'He's standing on one leg.'

'He's much better than this morning,' said Carla.

'Oh, he's always been able to do that,' said a voice behind them. 'He's been riding since he was two.'

Adam, Sue and Carla turned round. Alex was sitting
in the row behind them. But when they turned back
to look at the boy riding the horse they saw that
was Alex too.

'Alex!' gasped Adam. 'What's happened? How can you
be here and there at the same time?'

'I'm sorry,' laughed Alex. 'I'm afraid we've been
playing a trick on you. The boy in the ring is my
twin brother Tog.'

The audience clapped and cheered as Tog got off the
horse and went back to his new friends.

This is a picture of Tog and Alex. Look back through the story and see if you can work out which twin is which, and how they played the trick.

Which twin first opened the door?
Which twin spoke to Adam when he washed the car?
Which twin wore the wellingtons and went to the farm?
Which twin went to the circus?

Stories about twins

For hundreds of years people have been telling
stories about twins. One of the earliest is the
legend of Romulus and Remus, the twins who are
supposed to have built the city of Rome.

Romulus and Remus

Romulus and Remus were the twin sons of the god Mars.
A jealous king tried to drown the babies but they were
found by a she-wolf who brought them up with her cubs.
When they grew up, the boys fought a battle with the
king who had tried to harm them, and conquered his
lands. The boys decided to build a great city but
they could not decide who should be king of it.
They fought each other and Romulus won and named
the city Rome. It's strange to think that if Remus
had won, the city we call Rome might have been
called Reme!

Castor and Pollux

If you were born between May 21st and June 21st your star sign is Gemini, the twins. You may not know the legend of the Gemini twins. It's a strange one. The twins' father was Zeus, chief of the Greek gods who turned himself into a swan. The twins' mother laid two eggs. Out of one hatched Helen of Troy, the most beautiful woman in the world. Out of the other hatched Castor and Pollux, the twins.

Castor and Pollux grew up into great heroes. Castor was made god of horse-racing and Pollux became god of boxing. Zeus wanted his sons to live in the sky with him forever so he turned them into stars.

Famous twins

Do you recognise these famous twins?

Biff and Chip.

Tweedle Dum and Tweedle Dee.

The Emperor's lesson

Many hundreds of years ago lived an Emperor called
Justinian. He was very rich but he was also very
mean. The only thing that interested him was
himself. Justinian had twenty cooks in the palace
and they spent all their time inventing new and
exciting meals that might please him. He never wore
the same clothes more than once. While he slept his
twenty tailors had to make the rich garments that he
would wear on the following day.

Do you think Justinian was happy? He was not.
He was always bored and bad tempered. If he didn't
like the food he was given, he would scream and shout
and throw it on the floor. If he did not like the
clothes his tailors made for him he would tear them
into bits. The truth is he was spoilt.

One day a group of poor people came to the palace
to ask the Emperor for help. The winter had been
long and cold and they did not have enough to eat.
The taxes they paid to the Emperor were so heavy
that they could not afford bread to feed their children.
The captain of the guard went to Justinian
and told him there were people at the palace gate
asking to see him.

'What people?' asked Justinian crossly.

'Your subjects, sire,' said the captain.

'Send them away. They make the place look untidy.'

'But they say they are starving, sire.'

'So am I,' laughed Justinian. 'I've had nothing to eat
since breakfast. Go and get my lunch and send
those peasants away at once.'

After lunch Justinian decided to go hunting. He and his huntsmen spent the afternoon chasing wild boar, but they didn't catch any. Tired and exhausted, Justinian threw himself down on the banks of a river and ordered his men to prepare the picnic they had brought with them. 'While you're getting things ready, I think I shall have a dip in this delightful river,' said Justinian. 'I hope you remembered to bring the big towel. If you didn't there will be trouble.' He took off his clothes and dived into the warm water.

When Justinian had splashed about for a bit he swam
back to the bank. There was no sign of the huntsmen,
the picnic, or his clothes. The Emperor was furious.

'If you're playing a joke on me,' he shouted. 'You
will find I'm not amused. Where are you hiding?
Come out at once!' But there was nobody there.

Justinian found an old sack to wrap around himself
and walked back to the palace. When he got there he
was cold and tired and dirty.

'Where do you think you're going?' asked a guard.

'I'm going to have a bath and then put some clothes
on and then I'm going to throw all my huntsmen into
a deep, dark, smelly dungeon,' shouted the Emperor.

'Oh yes,' smiled the guard, 'and who are you?'

'I'm your Emperor!' screamed Justinian. But the
guards just laughed and laughed.

'This is your lucky day,' smiled the guard. 'Our Emperor came back from hunting an hour ago. He gave orders that all his poor subjects were to be invited to a great feast. I don't know who you are but I expect you're welcome to come in too.'

'But don't you recognise me?' asked Justinian.

'Never seen you before in my life,' said the guard. Justinian dashed into the palace and ran towards his bedroom. He was stopped by a soldier. 'You can't go in there,' said the soldier. 'Those are the Emperor's rooms. You belong in the hall with the other beggars.'

'But don't you know who I am?' asked Justinian. By now he was becoming frightened. 'I'm the Emperor.'

The soldier laughed. 'I think you must be a madman. I've served the Emperor for ten years and he wouldn't go about dressed like you. At this moment he's getting changed for the banquet. If you behave yourself and go along to the great hall they'll give you a good feed. If you don't I'll have you thrown out.'

Justinian rushed to the great hall. There were several of his courtiers there but none of them recognised him. In a rage he jumped on a table. 'Look at me,' he cried. 'Don't any of you know me? I'm your Emperor!' The courtiers began to laugh. So did the poor people sitting at the tables. Justinian began to cry.

At that moment the doors of the great hall opened and a man walked into the room. The man was wearing Justinian's crown and clothes. Justinian could hardly believe his eyes. It was as if he were looking at himself in a mirror. The man was his double. When the man spoke it was with Justinian's own voice. 'Take that madman away from here,' he said, 'and throw him in the dungeon.'

Justinian was so shocked that he fainted.

When Justinian came to his senses he found himself
in his own bedroom. There was a strange glow in the
room and the man who was his double stared down
at him.

'You are wicked and selfish,' said the stranger.
'You have been given great wealth and power but you
have also been given the task of looking after your
people. You waste all your time and money on idle
pleasures whilst your people starve. If you don't
mend your ways your kingdom will be taken from
you and given to somebody who will rule it well.'
With that, the man disappeared.

From that day Justinian was a changed man. He
ruled his empire wisely and well. His people grew
prosperous and happy. Justinian was happy too
because he now had something far more important
than all his wealth, and that was friends.